THE SOUND BITES

AMY GRACE ULMAN, MS, CCC/SLP

ILLUSTRATIONS BY AMY SOLARO

ISBN 13: 978-1-954020-01-6

Printed in the United States of America on acid-free paper

10 9 8 7 6 5 4 3 2 1
First Edition

Part of the Tree Neutral® program, which offsets the
number of trees consumed in the production and printing
of this book by taking proactive steps, such as planting
trees in direct proportion to the number of trees used:
www.treeneutral.com

TreeNeutral®

For Clara and Sam, whose voices are my
favorite sounds in the world.

The Sound Bites were simply doing what they do best. **Talking.**
While doing what they love most. **Eating.**

Each one an instrument of their own unique sound.
Together, a symphony of chatter.

Bob

Pop

Willis

Hank

Mimi

Nana

Coco

Gus

Titus

Dudley

Inga

Rupert

Frank

Yeller

Leo

The whole crew was there.
Even the vowels—
they can never be left out.

Chuck

Spencer

Shay

Zoey

Joey

Viv

Thou

Theo

Zsa-Zsa

Al

Ed

Ike

Oz

Ugg

The Sound Bites were chuckling about chickpeas, gabbing about gumbo, and blabbing about baked beans.

And then . . . it happened.

The classic supper switcharoo: parents order salads but steal their kid's meal.

The Sound Bites had seen this one too many times.
Why couldn't kids just have their own food?

A menu they could count on.
Owned and operated by kids alone.
It was time to help kids reclaim their plates.

The Sound Bites were the perfect bunch
to take on the Kids' Menu mission!

They pondered, puzzled,
projected, and planned.

They fiddled, fixed, figured,
and finally found . . .

. . . THE five legendary foods
that would officially belong
to all children everywhere!

Each **m**outhful of this **m**agical, **m**ystery **m**eat **m**elts in your **m**outh.

I could **n**ibble **n**on-stop, **n**oon, or **n**ight, then **n**estle in for a **n**ice **n**ap.

Whether it's **w**inter or **w**arm **w**eather, it's **w**ieners for the **w**in!

No more **t**ears or **t**emper **t**antrums when **t**iny **t**oddlers **t**aste this **t**oasty **t**reasure.

I'll si**ng** for the zi**ng** of this yummy thi**ng**, just pi**ng** me or give me a ri**ng**-a-di**ng**-di**ng**!

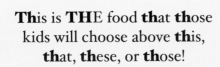

This is **TH**E food **th**at **th**ose kids will choose above **th**is, **th**at, **th**ese, or **th**ose!

Vendors will deliver to a **v**ariety of **v**enues, which is a **v**ery **v**aluable **v**irtue indeed.

Here's a **th**ought, **th**row out the **th**awed turkey and **th**ermometer and have pizza for a **Th**anksgiving **th**rill!

Behold. The Kids' Menu was born!

The Sound Bites went bananas!

They went nuts.
They thought the Kids' Menu was the
greatest thing since sliced bread . . .

So, they toasted with toast . . .

. . . did the cha-cha with chips . . .

. . . and dipped with dips.

It was a classic Sound Bites
celebration!

As for the grown-ups, the Sound Bites all agreed;
They may enjoy some bites from the Kids' Menu too
(just as long as they clean their plates first).

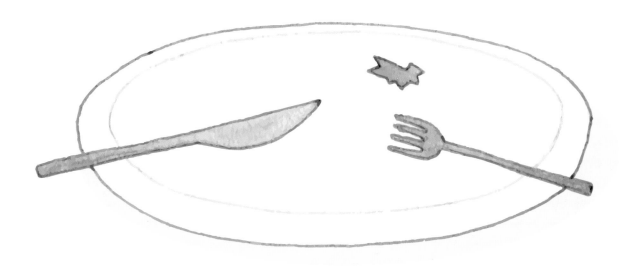

And maybe—just maybe—they will share a bite of their
simple yet super scrumptious salad with the kids.

TIPS TO PROMOTE SPEECH &

Read with your child everyday.

Name and describe pictures. Ask open-ended questions.

Maintain eye contact when talking to your child.

Let your child see your mouth movements while talking and playing with sounds.

Encourage your child to use gestures or signs to communicate.

Throughout your day, narrate what you are doing or what your child is doing.

Treat your child as a full communication partner. Take turns communicating.
Acknowledge what was said, even if it's babbling.

Resist the urge to anticipate your child's wants/needs.
Instead, allow your child the chance to communicate.

LANGUAGE DEVELOPMENT AT HOME

Give it time. Wait at least 5-10 seconds for your child to respond.

Turn off the background TV. Limit distractions while communicating.

Repeat back what your child says, and expand it by adding detail.

Ask open-ended questions rather than yes/no questions.

(Example: "Where did you go?" instead of "Did you go to the park?")

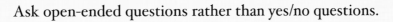

When your child makes an incorrect speech sound, simply repeat back what was said using

the correct pronunciation without overtly correcting.

Stay positive! Reinforce what your child is already doing and celebrate those skills.

Again, keep reading!

The Sound Bites book focuses on the 24 consonant sounds used in English, presented in the order in which children typically acquire those sounds.

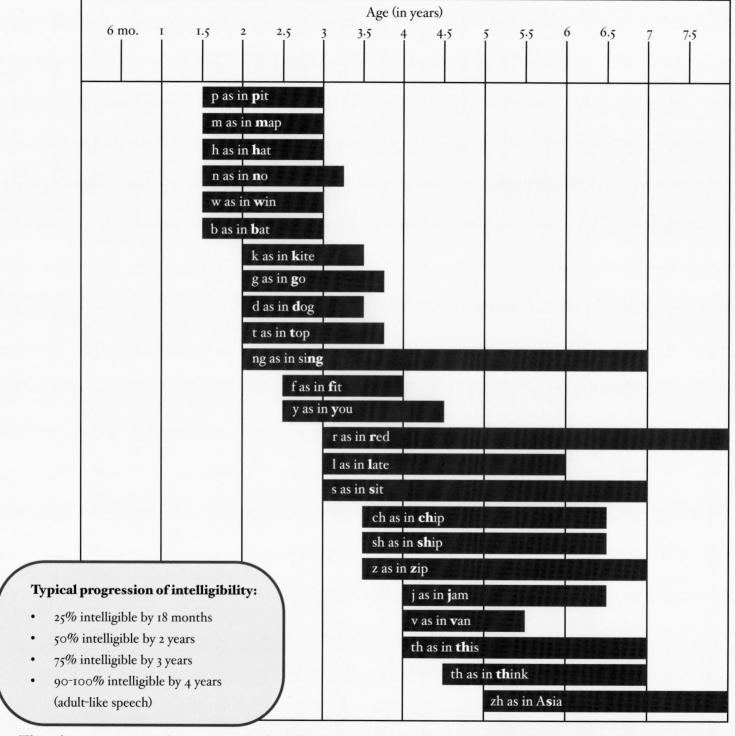

Typical progression of intelligibility:

- 25% intelligible by 18 months
- 50% intelligible by 2 years
- 75% intelligible by 3 years
- 90-100% intelligible by 4 years (adult-like speech)

This chart represents the ages at which children typically develop speech sounds in English. Each bar starts at the age when 50% of children have mastered that sound and ends at the age when 90% of children have mastered that sound. This chart is based on the combined data of Sander (1972), Grunwell (1981), and Smit et al. (1990).

LETTER TO PARENTS

Did you know that using speech to communicate is one of the most complex things that we do as human beings? Yet it is something we don't usually think about.

Until we need to.

My first child was an early talker. My second child was a late talker. That was not part of the plan. I was a working speech-language pathologist, yet somehow this caught me off guard and I felt unsure of myself. The questions ensued. *Is this my fault? Did I give my first child more attention? If I seek help, am I admitting there is a problem?* And then the deepest darkest question that will make my speech therapy colleagues' hair stand on end . . . *would speech therapy really help?* There, I said it. When faced with the communication challenges of my own child, I had all of those thoughts, and I know the research! I know the answers. It is amazing what our worried minds will do when it comes to our children—from avoiding confronting a challenge to inventing one that doesn't exist. Was I falling into either of these traps? My knowledge of the vast benefits of early intervention prevailed and we pursued help. When my child graduated from speech therapy talking up a storm, my eyes were opened to the power of early intervention in a new way because, for the first time, I was seeing it through the lens of a parent.

There is so much more to speech and language development than acquiring sounds. This book is a starting point in bringing that complex thing we do, called speech, to a new level of awareness. My hope is that you and your child will think about and have fun with speech sounds, and appreciate that sounds develop over time and in an often predictable order. Sometimes we worry unnecessarily about our kiddos' development, and sometimes it is time to get extra support by a licensed professional. Whether we are worried or not, there are steps we can all take at home to foster speech and language development. If I, a speech therapist, had questions and trepidation about taking the next step, how might other parents be feeling? Be empowered to take the next step, whatever it might be, with confidence. Life is complex enough, setting our kids up for success doesn't have to be.

– AMY GRACE ULMAN

If you have concerns about your child's speech and language development, or physical development, talk to your pediatrician. Early Intervention programs exist in every state and territory in the U.S. for children from birth to 3 years old, and these services are offered for free or reduced cost (regardless of household income). You do not need a referral from a doctor to get an evaluation. You can contact the Early Intervention program in your area and request an evaluation. For children ages 3–5, services are provided free of charge through the public school system (regardless if your child attends or will attend that school). Again, a doctor's referral is not required to access these services. You can contact your local public elementary school directly.